Bonkers

IT WASN'T ME!

With special thanks to Rachel Elliot

G.A.

ORCHARD BOOKS
338 Euston Road, London NW1 3BH
Orchard Books Australia
Level 17/207 Kent Street, Sydney, NSW 2000

First published in 2012 by Orchard Books

ISBN 978 1 40831 472 2

Text © Giles Andreae 2012
Cover illustration © Nick Sharratt 2012
Inside illustrations © Orchard Books 2012

The right of Giles Andreae to be identified as the author
of this work has been asserted by him in accordance
with the Copyright, Designs and Patents Act, 1988.

A CIP catalogue record for this book is available from the British Library.

3 5 7 9 10 8 6 4 2

Printed in Great Britain

Orchard Books is a division of Hachette Children's Books,
an Hachette UK company.

www.hachette.co.uk

Billy Bonkers

IT WASN'T ME!

Giles Andreae

ORCHARD

Giles Andreae is an award-winning
children's author who has written many
bestselling picture books, including
Giraffes Can't Dance and *Commotion in the Ocean*.

He is probably most famous as the creator of
the phenomenally successful Purple Ronnie,
Britain's favourite stick man. Giles lives by the river
near Oxford with his wife and four young children.

Contents

Billy Bonkers

and the
Painting Pinchers

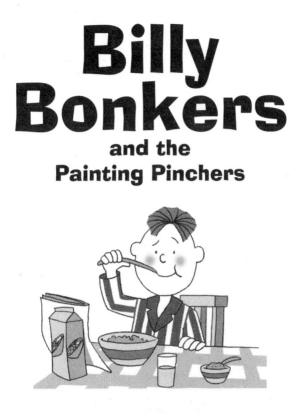

William Benedict Bertwhistle Bonkers took a large mouthful of dry porridge oats and let out a happy sigh. It was the start of half-term week, and Billy's first morning of freedom.

I don't know about you, but William – or Billy, as most people called him – preferred to start his free mornings with a few hours of comic-reading and follow that up with some action-packed computer gaming and a lot of snacking. However, this morning something was different. His comic was propped up against the orange juice carton, but he wasn't reading it. Instead his eyes were fixed on the headline that ran across the front page of his dad's newspaper, printed in big, bold, black letters.

* Town Herald *

SECRET PRANKSTER STRIKES AGAIN

"I wonder who the Secret Prankster is," said Billy's sister, Betty.

"You two should be thinking about your holiday homework, not that silly town joker," said Mrs Bonkers.

Billy grinned and took another mouthful of dry porridge oats. (Most people like their oats wet and cooked, but not Billy.) "I think he's brilliant, whoever he is," he said.

"How do you know it's a HE?" demanded Betty. "Could be a SHE."

"He OR she is nothing but a Massive Menace," said Mr Bonkers, rustling his newspaper. "Practical jokes being played on innocent people day and night. Police baffled. Town's gone mad."

"What's your homework, anyway?" asked Betty, who was weirdly interested in things like that.

"'What I Did During Half Term'," said Billy. "The most unbelievably boring homework assignment ever."

"That's the only homework Mr Little ever sets," said Betty.

The letterbox rattled and Mrs Bonkers went into the hall to pick up the post. Betty leaned over and turned up the volume on the radio.

"Time for our phone-in slot," said the high-pitched, high-speed voice of radio presenter Daisy Diggle. *"And today we're discussing the subject that's on everyone's lips – who IS the Secret Prankster?*

The Painting Pinchers

*Our first caller is Norman from Old Drain Street.
What do you want to say, Norman?"*

"That Secret Prankster let off a stink bomb in
the middle of my knitting club," snapped an
angry man's voice. "Somebody has to stop him!
We can't get the smell out of our bobble hats!"

"Disgraceful,"
muttered Mr
Bonkers, as Billy
snorted with
laughter and
sprayed bits of
porridge across
the table.

"Hi Daisy!" said the next caller. "My name's
Crystal and I'm a model. The Secret Prankster
balanced a bucket of paint over my front door
last weekend, and I've been walking around all
week coloured snot green. No one wants a snot-
green model!"

Mrs Bonkers tutted as she walked back into the kitchen with the post.

"Whoever it is, they're very naughty," she said, looking through the letters. "Bills, bills, junk mail . . . ooh – this one's from an art gallery in Italy. How odd."

"*Well, this Secret Prankster is certainly causing a ton of trouble in town,*" gabbled Daisy Diggle as Mrs Bonkers opened the letter. "*We've had cold-porridge bombs dropped on heads and bananas stuck in car exhausts. What's next, lovely listeners? The police are baffled. Do you know who the Secret Prankster is? Ring in and give us your guesses, guys!*"

"Cold porridge?" repeated Mr Bonkers, looking at Billy.

"It wasn't me!" said Billy in an indignant voice.

He stopped listening to the gabbling voice of Daisy Diggle, and drifted off into a daydream where  he became a world-famous detective, found the Secret Prankster and turned him over to the police.

"Lordy lorks!" squealed Mrs Bonkers, dropping the letter she was reading and putting her hands over her heart. "Oh, Sausage!"

Sausage was what Mrs Bonkers called Mr Bonkers most of the time. When she called him by his real name, he knew he was in trouble.

Billy Bonkers

Betty jumped out of her seat and picked up the letter. "Dear Bonkers family," she read out. "Congratulations! You have won the star prize in our draw – a two-day family holiday in Venice, Italy. You will visit the most famous painting in the world, the *Ghastly Groaner*, and then attend a fancy-dress ball at the Grand Gallery."

"WE WON!"

cried Mr Bonkers,
leaping out of his seat
and punching the air.
"WE'RE WINNERS!"
(He was a competitive
sort of person.)

"It's that competition I entered," said Mrs Bonkers. "I saw it on the back of a cereal packet and sent in our names. How exciting! When do we leave, Betty?"

Betty looked at the letter again and her eyes opened very wide.

"Oh my goodness!" she said. "The flight is this morning at ten o'clock!"

She peered at the envelope.

"Look, they sent it to the wrong address!" she added, waving it under her mother's nose. "It had to be redirected – that's why it's arrived late!"

"We'll never pack in time!" Mrs Bonkers exclaimed. "It's already seven o'clock! And there's so much to remember: passports, pants, socks, changes of clothes, medical kit, travel alarm, travel plug, bags, shoes, umbrellas, macs—"

"Stop panicking, Mum," said Betty. "The

airport's only half-an-hour's drive away."

For the next half-hour, the house was in uproar.

Mr Bonkers dived into the cupboard under the stairs to find his binoculars and bird-spotting books.

Betty packed a selection of maps, books and clothes in neat piles.

Mrs Bonkers picked out her fluffy slippers, her comfiest pants and a large number of outfits in case of rain, sun, snow or blizzards. It was only after she had sat on her suitcase to close it that she thought about hunky gondoliers. She opened the case again and added her favourite perfume, some face powder and a red lipstick.

Billy packed the bare necessities into his rucksack:

one change of clothes,

 his games console,

his new walkie-talkies,

 a bag of emergency sweets

and five pork pies.

Ten minutes later, the Bonkers family drove away from the house.

Fifteen minutes later, they drove back so that Mrs Bonkers could check that she had turned off the oven. She put a note through next door's letterbox asking them to feed her plants and Billy's goldfish, Snapper, and then they set off again. Italy didn't know what was about to hit it.

***

The pigeons in Venice don't get much peace. Don't get me wrong, they're not complaining. They like all the food and the attention.

(Venetian pigeons are the most photographed pigeons in the world, and some of them get a little bit proud and snooty about it.)

Anyway, the point is that when the busy season has ended and most of the tourists have gone home, the pigeons like to sit beside the canals and enjoy the peace.

"Oh, lordy lorks!" squealed a high-pitched voice, shattering the silence.

The pigeons rose up in a panicky mob of fluff and feathers as the Bonkers family slid into view, squashed into a small gondola.

"This is the life, Piglet!" said Mr Bonkers, leaning back in the gondola with his hands clasped behind his head.

Piglet was Mr Bonkers's pet name for Mrs Bonkers. Billy and Betty only minded when he used it in public.

"Mmm," said Mrs Bonkers, who was gazing up at the hunky, bronzed gondolier.

"Look at the buildings!" said Mr Bonkers. "The canals! The boats!"

"They're called gondolas, Dad," said Betty, whose nose was buried in a guidebook.

"Absolutely splendid," murmured Mrs Bonkers, who hadn't taken her eyes off the gondolier.

Billy was watching the gondolier too. First he lowered his long pole until it hit the muddy bottom of the canal. Then he pushed down on it to propel his gondola along. Then he pulled it out of the mud and started all over again.

"Brilliant!" said Billy. "I'd love to try that." (He said that last part under his breath, because he had a funny feeling that if he mentioned it, his parents might forbid it.)

The Painting Pinchers

The gondola drew up to a small landing platform and the Bonkers family stepped out. Their legs felt a little bit like cooked spaghetti, but they were all too excited to care.

"Time for some shopping!" said Mrs Bonkers, her eyes sparkling. "Everyone needs to choose a fancy-dress costume to hire for the ball."

Mrs Bonkers didn't really care about the *Ghastly Groaner* part of the prize. She just wanted to get dressed up and go to a posh party.

"Couldn't we go in a gondola again?" Billy asked.

"Later," said Mr Bonkers. "Aha, there's the costume shop! Come on, Piglet!" He hurried off, beckoning Mrs Bonkers to follow.

The shop was on the edge of a square, and it had lots of exciting-looking outfits in the window. The Bonkers family crowded inside and pushed their way through tightly packed rows of colourful costumes to a polished wooden counter.

A short, white-haired man beamed at them over half-moon glasses.

"Hello!" he said. "Are you looking for costumes?"

Mr and Mrs Bonkers nodded.

"We're going to the fancy-dress ball tonight at the Grand Gallery," Mrs Bonkers explained.

The man's smile faded.

"Haven't you heard?" he gasped. "The *Ghastly Groaner* has been stolen! The gallery is going to cancel the ball if it's not found."

"Oh, Sausage!" wailed Mrs Bonkers. "What are we going to do?"

Mr Bonkers put his arm around her.

"There, there, Piglet," he said. "Let's get costumes anyway. We can dress up even if there isn't a ball."

Billy thought that this sounded like a terrible idea. However, Mrs Bonkers brightened up considerably.

"I've already seen the perfect costume for me," she said, seizing an outfit from the rack nearest to her. It was a bright-green Lycra bodysuit covered in red and purple hoops that bounced up and down.

Billy and Betty took one look at it and exchanged horrified glances.

You've probably been embarrassed by your parents at some point, so I expect you can imagine how they felt at that moment. Although it did probably happen to Billy and Betty a little more often than it happens to you.

"Oh well," said Billy, who liked to try to look on the bright side. "At least Mum will be happy either way. But I do hope they find the painting."

"What about you two?" asked Mrs Bonkers. "There are some lovely costumes here. You could be a giant rabbit or a glow-in-the-dark penguin or—"

"This will be fine for me," said Billy, grabbing a pirate costume from the rack beside him.

"I'll be a witch," added Betty, picking up a black cape and pointed hat before her mother could suggest anything else. "Simple."

Mr Bonkers was finding it hard to make up his mind. He held up a giant orange parrot costume in one hand and a purple stripy starfish costume in the other. "How about one of these?" he asked.

"Mmm, they're a bit understated," said Mrs Bonkers.

Betty clapped her hands over her eyes and let out an exasperated sigh.

"Let's get out of here," Billy said to her.

Billy and Betty slipped out of the shop just as Mr Bonkers was climbing into a Christmas tree costume, complete with flashing lights.

The Painting Pinchers

Billy stopped beside a canal, took his walkie-talkies out of his rucksack and handed one to Betty. Betty opened her mouth as if to argue with him, but Billy interrupted her.

"I just want to see how far apart they'll work," he pleaded. "You go over to the far side of the square, and I'll stand here on the edge of the canal."

"Not now, Billy!" Betty replied. "I've just spotted a classic example of Byzantine architecture."

She bustled off towards the boring remains of a ramshackle old building, still clutching the walkie-talkie. Billy was left standing on his own beside the canal. And that's when he noticed the empty gondola.

Wouldn't it be brilliant, said a tiny little voice in his head, *if the gondolier had left it there especially for you?*

Billy took a step towards the boat.

You only need to take it a little way out, said the voice. *Just enough to try it. You won't do any harm. You'll be back before anyone even notices.*

If you're thinking that Billy shouldn't have been listening to that little voice, then you'd be quite right. But you see, Billy isn't very good at resisting things. For example, he can seldom resist a toffee apple. He can hardly ever resist one of Mrs Bonkers's pork pies. And he can absolutely, categorically never resist temptation.

Anyway, when he was faced with an empty gondola, his conscience didn't even put up a fight. He slipped the walkie-talkie into his pocket. Then he stepped down into the boat, untied it from the landing stage, picked up the pole and pushed off into the middle of the canal.

The part where he lowered the pole down to the muddy bottom of the canal went quite well. He pushed down on it, just as he had seen the gondolier do, and felt it sink into the mud at the bottom of the canal just as he expected it to. Then he leaned against the pole and pushed the gondola forwards. That part went fine too.

It was the next part, when he tried to pull the pole out of the mud, where things started to go wrong.

Instead of Billy being in charge of the pole, it turned out that the pole was in charge of Billy. It had no intention of coming out of the sticky mud. The harder he pulled on it, the deeper it seemed to get wedged. Meanwhile, the gondola glided on. But Billy was concentrating so hard on tugging the pole out of the mud that he didn't notice this until the gondola had glided right out from under him, leaving him clinging to the pole in the middle of the canal.

I don't think this is going to end well, thought Billy.

The trouble was (apart from the fact that he now had no gondola), that the pole was slippery, and Billy's hands were slippery, and as a result Billy's bottom was slowly inching closer and closer to the cold, dark water.

Just at the moment when it seemed as if he was going to have an unexpected bath, Billy heard the low growl of an engine. He whipped his head around and saw a speedboat cruising through the water towards him.

It was his only chance.

Billy took a deep breath and launched himself through the air toward the passing boat, dive-bombing into the back of it with a painful **CRUMP!**

There were three men in the front of the speedboat, and they all had their backs to him. The noise of the engines had drowned out his landing, and they hadn't noticed his entrance.

The Painting Pinchers

Billy opened his mouth to call out, but at that moment the boat did what speedboats do and picked up the pace. As its engine revved, its nose rose out of the water, and Billy was thrown backwards. He did three somersaults and crashed into something hard and rectangular.

Billy shook his head and blinked a few times. Then he looked around and found himself staring at something very familiar.

Billy's mouth fell open. If anyone could have seen him at that moment, the word "gormless" would have seemed a very apt description.

He was looking at a painting of an ugly, frowning young woman dressed in black. In fact, it was one of the most famous paintings in the world.

"The Ghastly Groaner!" Billy gasped.

He thought fast. *These men must be the thieves!* He crouched down behind the *Ghastly Groaner* and looked towards the front of the boat. They had half turned their heads, and he could see that each man was wearing a fancy-dress mask. One was disguised as Winston Churchill, another was William Shakespeare and the third was Queen Elizabeth II. Billy's adventure had taken a very sinister turn.

Suddenly, Billy's walkie-talkie crackled in his pocket. Billy nearly jumped out of his skin. He pulled it out and turned down the volume.

"*Billy?*" came Betty's voice. "*Where are you?*"

"Betty!" said Billy, crouching down lower and whispering into the walkie-talkie. "You'll never in a billion years guess what's just happened to me."

He explained his situation as fast as he could.

"*Wait a minute,*" said Betty. "*Let me check my map.*"

"Betty, this isn't a time for sightseeing!" Billy exclaimed.

"*Listen,*" said his sister. "*I think I might have an idea. I'm right beside the canal, and there are loads of gondoliers here. If I can get some of them to block the canal, we can stop the thieves escaping, rescue you and save the painting!"*

Billy peered out from behind the painting. The water divided into two separate canals ahead, and the boat was heading towards the right-hand one.

"There are two canals!" Billy cried into the walkie-talkie. "Which one are you talking about?"

There was an excruciatingly long pause while Betty consulted her map.

"The left canal," she said. *"If they take the other one they'll escape, and they'll take you with them! You've got to get them to head down the left one!"*

The Painting Pinchers

Billy shoved the walkie-talkie back into his pocket and looked at the thieves again. They all looked quite small and weedy, but he was outnumbered three to one. How was he supposed to stop them?

I've got a bad feeling about this, he thought.

Just then, his eyes fell on a fourth mask, which was lying beside the painting in the back of the boat. It carried the face of Elvis Presley. And that's when the Wonderful Plan sprang into Billy's mind.

Now, I expect you know that the key thing in an emergency is not to think too hard about what you're doing. If Billy had thought carefully about his plan at that moment, he wouldn't have gone through with it. Instead he would have jumped into the canal and hoped that he could remember how to doggy paddle. But he didn't think at all. He just put the mask over his face, jumped out from behind the painting and raced up to the front of the boat.

"The police are right behind us!" he yelled. "We have to change the route! Quick, go left!"

"**Police?**" screamed Winston Churchill. "*Let's get out of here!*" wailed William Shakespeare.

The Painting Pinchers

In a panic, Queen Elizabeth hauled on the steering wheel and the speedboat veered down the left-hand canal.

Then Shakespeare scratched his head.  "*Hang on a minute,*" he said slowly. "*I thought there were only three of us?*"

Uh-oh, thought Billy. *Perhaps I should have thought this through.*

Luckily for Billy, the thieves weren't much taller than him. It wasn't easy to tell which one of them was the odd one out.

"There's one too many on board!" said Winston Churchill. **"Who are you?"** He prodded Queen Elizabeth in the chest.

"**No names or faces!**" yelled Queen Elizabeth, putting up his fists. "**We agreed!**"

As all three men started to shout, Billy squeezed between Shakespeare's legs and looked out over the front of the speedboat. In the distance, but getting rapidly bigger, was a blockade of gondolas. Betty had worked fast!

The thieves were wrestling now, rolling around in the bottom of the boat and accusing one another of being a policeman in disguise.

"Billy!" crackled Betty's voice over the walkie-talkie. *"I can see you! Slow the boat down or you'll crash!"*

"I DON'T KNOW HOW!" Billy wailed.

Just then, Churchill hurled Shakespeare backwards onto the controls. He fell against a large silver lever, pushing it up hard. Instantly, the speedboat accelerated to top speed, leaping almost completely out of the water.

"**TOO FAST!**" screamed Queen Elizabeth.

The boat swung around violently. Billy fell sideways, grabbing onto the steering wheel to stop him falling over. As he did so, he wrenched it to the left. The boat swerved away from the blockade of gondolas,

missing them by inches, and smashed into
the wooden dock at the side of the canal
with a thudding

Its engine gave one last spluttering groan
and then died.

Billy looked up and saw Betty peering
down at him from the side of the canal.
There were six burly policemen behind her.

"Voila!" she said.

Now, I'm sure you haven't forgotten that
Billy was wearing the Elvis Presley mask.

Betty, of course, recognised her brother by his clothes and his hair, which was standing on end. The police, on the other hand, simply saw four people wearing masks.

Most policemen tend to be suspicious of people who wear masks. They also don't take kindly to people stealing paintings and smashing into docks, especially in Venice. After all, in a city that's mainly water, you need all the docks you've got.

Anyway, what the police saw was Billy standing behind the wheel, with three other men squirming around on the floor. You can't exactly blame them for jumping to the wrong conclusion. It really did look very much as if Billy was the ringleader.

"YOU'RE ALL UNDER ARREST!" shouted one of the policemen, producing a large pair of shiny handcuffs. "ESPECIALLY YOU!" he added, pointing at Billy.

shouted Billy.

"That's my brother!" yelled Betty.

The policemen weren't listening. They handcuffed Billy and the three thieves and marched them all onto dry land. Things weren't looking good.

But then the gondoliers started to shout from the water. Betty had told them all that Billy had been on board and found the painting. And if there's one thing you can say about gondoliers, it's that they have very, very, very loud voices.

"**Let Billy go!**"

"**He's a hero!**"

"**He saved the painting!**"

"Which one of them is Billy?" one of the police officers asked Betty.

"That one," Betty said, pointing at Elvis.

Reluctantly, the policeman who had arrested Billy undid his handcuffs. The gondoliers cheered, and Billy removed his mask and gave a bow.

"I guess I just did what I had to," he said modestly.

As the thieves were taken off to jail, Billy and Betty looked at each other.

"The fancy-dress ball is still on," said Billy happily. "Let's head back to the shop and tell Mum and Dad the good news."

But at that moment there was a loud squeal and Mrs Bonkers rushed up to them, clutching two big bags from the fancy-dress shop.

"Lordy lorks, Billy, what have you been doing?" she cried, dropping the bags and throwing her arms around him. "Police! Crooks! Whatever next?"

The Painting Pinchers

"Venice has gone mad," said Mr Bonkers, staring in amazement at all the gondoliers. "What's been going on, Billy?"

"It's a long story," said Billy with a grin. "We'll tell you all about it on the way to the fancy-dress ball."

"You mean it's going ahead?" said Mrs Bonkers. "Oh, Sausage, I can't wait! Let's look at our outfits again!"

As Mr and Mrs Bonkers pulled their garish costumes out of the bags and compared them admiringly, Betty turned to Billy.

"I've just thought of something else," she said. "Your homework assignment is going to be the most interesting one Mr Little's ever read!"

But Billy wasn't thinking about his homework. He wasn't even thinking about the fancy-dress ball. He was thinking how totally brilliant it would be if he could unmask the Secret Prankster when he got home.

If I can find a missing painting and three art thieves, he thought to himself, *I must be able to find one Secret Prankster. I'm going to be the best detective in town.*

He couldn't wait to get started!

THE END

Billy Bonkers

and the
Probability Machine

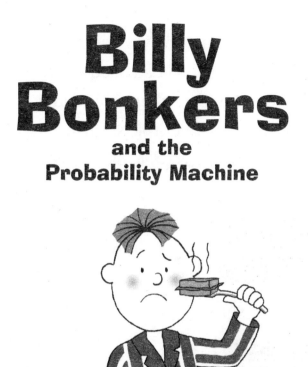

"I think Italy's gone to Mum's head," said Billy Bonkers. He stabbed at his overcooked lasagne with a fork.

"You like lasagne," said Betty.

"Not for breakfast," Billy pointed out.

They had only been back from Italy for twelve hours, and he was already missing it.

Catching the art thieves had been fun, and the fancy-dress ball had been awesome. Billy winced as he remembered his dad doing the twist dressed as a purple starfish. On second thoughts, perhaps some parts of it had been better than others...

"Lordy lorks!" said a large pile of laundry, bustling into the kitchen. "How can a two-day holiday mean a week's worth of washing?" The pile of laundry bent down beside the washing machine to reveal the tousled head of Mrs Bonkers. There was a loud rap on the back door, and the next-door

neighbours, Mr and Mrs Rocket, came in. Mr Rocket was looking sporty in a white tennis outfit. Mrs Rocket was wearing a pair of tight cycling shorts and jogging on the spot. Mr Bonkers  felt a dizzy spell coming on.

"Morning!" boomed Mr Rocket. "How was Italy?"

"Well," said Mrs Bonkers, "we had a lovely…"

"Fantastic, marvellous!" said Mr Rocket. "Not much has been happening while you've

been away. The Secret Prankster went very quiet. But funnily enough he struck again last night, just after you got back."

"What happened?" asked Betty.

"Mrs Furball's wig was filled with jam," said Mrs Rocket.

"Terrible business," added Mr Rocket. "Very sticky situation."

Mr Bonkers picked up the jam jar from the table. It was almost empty.

"Wasn't this full when we went on holiday?"

he asked, looking at Billy.

"Do you, er, know anything about Mrs Furball's wig, Billy?"

"It wasn't me!"

Billy exclaimed.

"I'm tired of hearing about the Secret Prankster, anyway," said Mrs Rocket. "I think we need something to take our minds off it."

"That's why we've decided to throw a murder mystery party," said Mr Rocket. "We're asking all the neighbours over. I'll be playing Lord Bertram Blenkinsop."

"And I'll be Lady Blenkinsop," added Mrs Rocket, tossing back her hair. "Everyone will have a part to play."

Billy thought that this all sounded a bit silly. On the other hand, he hadn't forgotten his plan to unmask the Secret Prankster. Perhaps he would find the culprit at the murder mystery party.

"Anyway, we just popped in to give you your invitations," said Mr Rocket.

He placed four cards on the table.

"The cards have the details of the characters you'll be playing," said Mrs Rocket. "Toodle-oo!"

As they left, Mr Bonkers picked up the top card and read the text on the envelope. His ears and the tip of his nose went very red.

"I don't believe it!" he exclaimed. "The cheek! The outrage! They've cast me as the butler!"

"Now, now, Sausage," said Mrs Bonkers, looking at her card. "It's just a bit of fun. I've got the part of the cook, see?"

As I expect you know, Mr Bonkers had a bit of a competitive streak. Actually, if he had been a stick of rock, he would have had the words 'I LIKE WINNING' written all the way through his middle.

"Well, I'm going to be the best butler they've ever seen," he announced. "No one's going to be able to take their eyes off me."

Knowing Dad, Billy thought, *that's probably true.*

"What's my part?" he asked.

"It just says that you're the 'son of the cook and butler'," said Mrs Bonkers, reading Billy's card. "But I'm not sure you should be allowed to go. Have you done all of your holiday homework?"

"I'll do it at the weekend," said Billy. "Lots of time yet. Oh, PLEASE, Mum!"

"Well, I suppose it is half-term," said Mrs Bonkers, wrestling a huge pile of pants into the washing machine. "All right, we'll all go."

"Excellent," said Billy.

He took his invitation from his mum and read it out loud.

Dear Billy,

Please come to our murder mystery party tonight. You will be playing the son of the cook and butler. Please dress up accordingly.

When you arrive, you will be given more information about your character. The aim of the game is to find the murderer, and the winner will receive a very special prize – a family ticket to the fairground for the whole weekend!

See you at the party!

Roger and Candy Rocket

While Billy had been reading, a glint had appeared in the eyes of Mr Bonkers. It was the sort of glint that appeared whenever there was a chance  that he might beat Mr Rocket at something.

"I'm going to get started on my costume right now," he said, leaping out of his seat. "And I've thought of just the gadget to help me win the prize!"

"Can I come, Dad?" asked Billy.

Billy thought that the gadget sounded like something he wanted to see. Mr Bonkers was a great inventor. At least, he was very good at thinking up ideas. Sometimes the actual gadgets didn't work out quite the way he had planned.

"Not just yet, Billy," said Mr Bonkers. "I need time alone to create."

Billy sighed as he watched his father gallop out to the shed. Mr Bonkers's shed was a very interesting though rather dangerous place, full of unexpected smells and random sounds. Billy loved it.

"Now what am I going to do all day?" Billy wondered aloud.

If you have ever said that sort of thing when your parents can hear you, I expect you have discovered what a terrible mistake it is. Billy realised his error as soon as he looked at his mother. She was wearing an expression that said: "I will have no problem finding all sorts of things for you to do."

Betty scraped her breakfast bowl clean and zoomed out of the kitchen before she could be involved in Billy's mistake.

"That's a very good question," said Mrs Bonkers, taking a deep breath. "First you can help me with the laundry, and then you can do the dusting while I do the vacuuming. And then you can clean out the goldfish bowl, tidy your bedroom, water the plants, mow the lawn, wash the car and start on the ironing."

"But—"

"Goats butt," said Mrs Bonkers, handing Billy a flowery apron and a feather duster. "Boys help out their mothers."

Billy didn't enjoy that day very much. Every time he looked out at the shed, he saw puffs of smoke escaping from between the planks, and flashes of electricity sparking in the windows. Whatever Mr Bonkers was up to, it was EPIC. And Billy was missing out.

CRASH!

ZZAAP!

BANG!

WHUMMP!

As the sun started to set, Billy finally finished tidying his room. He glanced out of the window and gasped. The shed door was opening! Mr Bonkers popped his head out and glanced around in a furtive manner. Then he looked up at Billy's bedroom window. Billy waved, and Mr Bonkers put his finger over his lips. Then he beckoned.

In a blur of dusters and flowery aprons, Billy hurtled downstairs and out to the shed. Five seconds later, he was staring up at his father.

For a moment, he didn't know what to say.

Mr Bonkers was now wearing a traditional butler's suit, but that was where tradition had decided to take a break and let loopiness take over. Instead of the usual black, his suit was bright yellow, and the collar and cuffs were

Bright yellow suit

Green sequins

Green sequins

decorated with green sequins. "How do I look?" asked Mr Bonkers. "Honestly?" asked Billy. Mr Bonkers nodded eagerly. A smile crept over Billy's face. "You look awesome," he said.

"I knew it!" declared Mr Bonkers. "Roger Rocket will rue the day he made me his butler!"

"But what's the amazing gadget?" asked Billy, who was dying to find out what his father had invented.

Mr Bonkers stepped to one side and revealed a small black box. It had a digital display that flashed random numbers and letters on the front, and lots of colourful buttons and knobs all over it. Mr Bonkers had snaffled a keypad from an old electronic musical toy  of Billy's and hooked it up to the machine. Billy loved it immediately. "It's BRILLIANT, Dad!" he said. "Um, what is it?"

"This, my boy," said Mr Bonkers, puffing out his chest with pride, "is my brand-new Probability Machine! All I have to do is enter the facts that we know into it and ask a question. Then it sorts the data and uses probability and statistics to work out the solution. I've been entering information into it all day."

"Sounds awesome!" said Billy.

The Probability Machine

"Look!" Mr Bonkers said as he tapped eagerly on the keyboard. It worked really well, but it was neon yellow and it played a different musical note for each letter of the alphabet. "I've just told it about your mother's cooking habits, and asked it to predict what we're having for tea tomorrow," he explained.

He pushed a button and the Probability Machine made a whizzing, popping sound, and then words appeared on the little screen:

BURNT
PORK PIES
PROBABILITY:
98%

"Amazing!" said Billy. His mind was racing.

If this machine could help his dad to figure out who the murderer was, maybe it could also work out the identity of the Secret Prankster.

The party will be a sort of test run, he decided.

He couldn't wait to begin!

***

The Bonkers family were the last party guests to arrive. They walked into the living room to find Mrs Rocket busily handing out cards to all the guests. She looked very elegant in a silver satin evening gown with ropes of pearls around her neck.

"These cards will tell you more about your characters," Mrs Rocket was saying. "Now, one of you will find out that you are the murderer, one of you is the detective and some of you are the victims."

"Ooh, I'm the detective!" said Betty, waving her card in the air. "I get to investigate and ask everyone questions!"

All the guests had dressed up, and there was a lot of laughter and excitement. Mr Rocket was handing around colourful drinks with little paper umbrellas in them, and Mr Bonkers was hiding in a corner, showing Billy how to enter data into the Probability Machine.

The game began when they heard a blood-curdling scream. Mrs Bonkers put her hands over her ears, but everyone else ran upstairs to find Mrs Rocket lying on

her bedroom floor, pretending to be dead.
She was very convincing.

Betty stepped
forward with an air of
bossiness. (If you have
an older sister, you will
know exactly what sort of expression she was
wearing.)

"Ladies and gentlemen, Lady Blenkinsop
has been murdered," she announced. "I shall
start questioning suspects immediately.

Please go downstairs and wait for me in the sitting room."

Billy watched Mr Bonkers add the details about the murder into the Probability Machine. Then he felt a firm hand on his arm.

"You can be my assistant, Billy," said Betty. "Come along and take notes for me."

"I'm in the middle of some very important calculations," Billy argued. "Take your own notes."

"Never mind that, Billy," said Mr Bonkers. "Go and help your sister."

With a deep sigh, Billy followed Betty into the sitting room. He was never going to find the Secret Prankster at this rate!

All the guests were standing and sitting around, looking excited. Mrs Rocket was there too, although she was now just an observer. Betty gave Billy a notepad and a pencil, and stepped up to Mrs Furball, who was playing a cat-loving foreign diplomat called Irma Ukulele.

"Where were you at the time of the murder, Miss Ukulele?" she began.

Something funny happens to Billy's brain when he's not interested in what's going on in front of him. It's as if it climbs out of his skull and wanders around looking for something better to think about. Sometimes, like when he's playing a computer game, it can be really useful. It might help him find hidden clues or entrances to other levels. At other times, like when Mr Little is teaching the class about fractions, it results in a visit to the headmaster's office. And when his older sister is expecting him to take notes for her, it really isn't a good idea to do anything but try very hard to concentrate.

The trouble was that Billy's brain really wasn't interested in which sofa Mrs Furball had been sitting on when she heard the scream. Instead, it started to wonder who the Secret Prankster might be. Mr Rocket, perhaps? Mrs Bonkers was always saying that he had a juvenile sense of humour. (Billy wasn't sure whether this was an insult or a compliment.) Or how about the fashion students who shared a flat down the road – Wanda and Hubert? The neighbours always said that they liked playing silly games.

He only realised that his thoughts had been wandering when he found his sister glaring

into his face. "You haven't written down a single word!" she complained. "Honestly, if you want something done properly, you really have to do it yourself."

Billy thought this was an excellent motto. He shoved the pad and pencil into Betty's hands and raced off to find his father.

Mr Bonkers handed the Probability Machine to Billy as soon as he saw him.

"Back in a jiffy," he said. "Keep that safe!"

As Mr Bonkers darted in the direction of the toilet in a blur of yellow and green, Billy crept into a quiet corner and quickly opened a brand-new file in the machine's memory.

The Probability Machine

Using the musical touch pad, he entered all the names of the people at the party, as well as their ages and descriptions of their characters. There was a lot of tuneful beeping, and he kept his fingers crossed that the other guests would be too busy to ask what was making all the noise.

Billy entered all the peculiar things that had been happening around the town. Then he typed in his question: "Who is the Secret Prankster?"

The machine whirred, and then the results appeared on the screen.

BILLY BONKERS PROBABILITY: 86%

"What?" exclaimed Billy.

"It wasn't me!"

He tried a different question. "Who did the secret pranks?"

Again the machine whirred, and again the answer popped up on screen.

*BILLY BONKERS
PROBABILITY: 94%*

"It WASN'T me!"

said Billy through gritted teeth.

He shook the machine and another message appeared on the screen.

YOU DUNNIT!

Billy was wondering whether to reset the whole machine and start again, or simply to destroy it, when there was a tremendous shriek from the sitting room. He raced in to find Mrs Rocket standing with her hands to her neck.

"MY PEARLS!" she wailed. "SOMEONE HAS STOLEN MY PEARLS!"

The ropes of pearls that had been around her neck earlier had completely vanished. Before anyone else could say a word, Betty stepped forward.

"The fake murder mystery has turned into a real-life robbery!" she announced, holding her finger aloft in a dramatic style. "Ladies and gentlemen, someone here is a jewel thief. I will unmask the robber!"

This detective role has gone straight to her head, Billy thought.

Just then, Mr Bonkers appeared in the doorway.

"Billy, use the Probability Machine!" he said in a loud whisper.

No way, thought Billy. *It'll probably say I did it!*

Meanwhile, Betty had created an interview desk at the kitchen table, so Billy went over to watch. One by one the party guests came through to be interrogated. They all had to empty their pockets and describe what they had been doing since hearing the scream.

Some of them were confused and forgetful, like Mrs Furball. She had three balls of wool and a cat collar in her pockets.

"I don't really know what I've been doing," she said, rather unhelpfully. "I think those colourful drinks have muddled my head up."

Some of them were jokey and relaxed, like Mr Rocket. He had a comb, a pocket mirror and a maid's apron in his pockets.

"Wife's got too much jewellery anyway," he said with a laugh.

"Very suspicious," Betty whispered to Billy.

Some of them were downright angry, like Mr Bonkers. He had a boiled sweet, five scratchcards and a doorknob in his pockets.

"Accused by my own offspring!" he roared. "You've both gone mad!"

Eventually, Betty had interviewed all the guests, but none of them would admit to taking the pearls, and none of them had anything that connected them to the robbery in their pockets. It was almost a complete waste of time.

I say almost, because Billy noticed one very useful thing. When Flopsy Fontwell, who ran the local bookshop, emptied her pockets, he spotted her murder mystery party card among the pens, pencils and screwed-up receipts. And he saw four words that were very interesting indeed:

You are the murderer!

"This is hopeless," said Mrs Rocket. "We're going to have to call the police."

"Wait a minute," said Betty. "There's one more thing I'd like to try. Mrs Rocket, will you retrace your steps from the moment you were murdered to the moment you realised the necklace was missing? It might just give us a clue."

Mrs Rocket sighed, but she went upstairs and lay down on her bedroom floor, on the rug beside the bed.

"I lay here and I screamed," she said. "That was it!"

Betty took out a magnifying glass.

"Where did you get that from?" asked Billy.

"Shhh!" said Betty.

She got down on the floor beside Mrs Rocket. Then she crept slowly around the floor, inch by inch, with her nose almost touching the carpet.

"Girl's gone mad," said Mr Bonkers, who was watching from the doorway.

"Aha!" exclaimed Betty as she reached the side of the bed. She put her hand under the bed ... and drew out a long string of pearls! "You've found them!" squealed Mrs Rocket, jumping to her feet. "How marvellous!"

"Simple, really," said Betty with a modest shrug. "If no one had stolen them, they must have come undone and fallen off when you were playing dead."

Everyone went back downstairs to carry on with the party. Billy slipped into the kitchen, hoping to find a spare sausage or three. And that's when he heard it.

The Probability Machine

"So who do you think the murderer is?" the fashion student called Wanda was asking Mr Bonkers.

"Aha," said Mr Bonkers, tapping his nose. "That'd be telling."

"You mean you know?" gasped Wanda, her eyes growing very big. "Ooh, you are clever, Mr Bonkers."

"He's just bluffing!" boomed Mr Rocket from across the kitchen. "A mere butler isn't going to figure this out! Especially one who's dressed up like a sparkly banana! Ha!"

Mr Bonkers's ears turned the colour of a beetroot.

Now, up until that moment, Billy had no intention of making use of the very useful thing he had discovered earlier. After all, it would be like cheating. But when he saw Mr Rocket laughing, and his father looking red and upset, cheating suddenly didn't seem like such a bad idea after all.

"There's as much chance of you winning this as there is of you winning the fathers' race on sports day," Mr Rocket added.

Billy thought that this was a particularly low blow.

I expect you have had moments where you wanted very much to see someone get exactly what they deserved. Well, the temptation to teach Mr Rocket a lesson was very, very strong. And as I think I have mentioned before, if there's one thing that Billy can't resist, it's temptation.

Right, said Billy to himself.

The Probability Machine

He quickly entered "Flopsy Fontwell is the murderer" into the Probability Machine. Then he raced after his dad.

"I think it's ready to come up with the answer now," he whispered, thrusting the machine into Mr Bonkers's hands.

"I don't know," sighed Mr Bonkers. "Maybe I'm just fooling myself."

"Just try it," Billy urged him.

With a sigh, Mr Bonkers typed in the question "Who is the murderer?" After a click and a whirr, the machine delivered its answer.

Mr Bonkers opened his eyes very wide. Then he marched into the sitting room and stood by

the mantelpiece. Everyone else was sitting down and looking at him in awe. It was at moments like these that he wished he smoked a pipe or wore a deerstalker hat.

"It is time for the truth to be revealed," he said in his best heroic voice.

"Ooh, Sausage!" gasped Mrs Bonkers, clasping her hands together.

Mr Bonkers gazed around the room.

The Probability Machine

"Everyone here had a motive for murder," he declared. "YOU, Irma Ukulele," he said, pointing at Mrs Furball, "wanted Lady Blenkinsop dead because, er . . . um . . ."

Billy groaned and felt his cheeks getting hot with embarrassment. The Probability Machine hadn't said anything about motives!

Luckily, Betty came to the rescue.

"Was it because Irma Ukulele is a secret assassin in the pay of a mysterious and shady organisation run by cats?" she asked.

"Exactly!" Mr Bonkers agreed. "But she wasn't the only suspicious character."

He pointed an accusing finger at Mr Rocket.

"YOU, Lord Blenkinsop, wanted your wife dead so that . . . er . . ."

"So he could marry the scullery maid," hissed Betty. "That's why he had her apron in his pocket!"

"Precisely!" said Mr Bonkers.

Billy, who had been holding his breath, let it out with a long

WHOOSH

and almost blew Mrs Furball's wig off. If his dad went on like this much longer, people would realise that he hadn't done any detective work at all! "So who DID murder Lady Blenkinsop?" he asked.

Thankfully, Mr Bonkers took the hint.

"The murderer is . . . Flopsy Fontwell!" he exclaimed, pointing at her.

There was a breathless pause, and Billy felt as if cubes of ice were dropping into his stomach one by one. What if he had somehow made a mistake?

Then Flopsy gave a girlish giggle. "You're absolutely right, Mr Bonkers," she said. "My, how clever of you to work it out!"

The game was over! There was a loud round of applause from all the guests.

"Three cheers for Mr Bonkers!" cried Wanda. "*Hip hip hooray! Hip hip hooray! Hip hip hooray!*"

Mrs Rocket presented Mr Bonkers with his prize and kissed him on the cheek. Mr Bonkers turned a deep crimson colour. Meanwhile, Mr Rocket was looking rather green around the gills.

Now, I am sure that you would never do anything so dreadful as to cheat during a murder mystery game. But then perhaps you don't have a neighbour like Mr Rocket. I'm afraid to say that Billy didn't feel at all ashamed of himself. In fact, there was only one thought occupying Billy's mind at that moment.

It wasn't Betty's amazing detective work.

It wasn't his holiday homework.

It wasn't even the Secret Prankster.

It was the fact that his father had just won a family ticket to the fairground for the whole weekend, and Billy knew for a fact that they had the scariest roller coaster in the country:

THE TRIPLE-LOOP STOMACH CHURNER

He couldn't wait for Saturday!

Billy
Bonkers
and the
Secret Prankster

"WOOOOOOHOOOOOOOOO!" shouted
Billy Bonkers as the Triple-Loop Stomach
Churner hurtled towards the ground.

"I can't watch!" squealed Mrs Bonkers,
who was standing below.

Billy had lost count of how many times
he had ridden this roller coaster over the

last two days. It still took his breath away. Sometimes it took the snacks he had eaten away as well. In fact, it advertised itself as being able to make more people vomit than any other ride.

When he wasn't focusing on keeping his food where it belonged, Billy had spent the weekend taste-testing the different types of candyfloss around the fairground. There were five stalls and nine colours to choose from. He had also won fifteen cuddly toys on the hoopla. Billy wasn't really a cuddly

toy sort of person, so he had given them all to his mother. Mrs Bonkers definitely was a cuddly toy sort of person, and she was immensely proud of how many Billy had won.

The Secret Prankster

Now it was the final evening of the Bonkers family's weekend at the fairground. They had certainly made the most of it. Billy had only been home to sleep, and even then he had dreamed about the fairground. Billy grinned as the roller coaster juddered to a stop.

"Wicked!" he said aloud.

"Oh, Billy," twittered Mrs Bonkers as he climbed out of the roller coaster and wobbled towards her. "You're so brave!"

"Brave?" repeated Betty, who had just wandered up carrying a goldfish in a bag of water. "Barmy, more like."

Billy would have liked to reply, but he was feeling a little bit sick. He decided to take a break from the roller coaster.

After all, he had just been around five times without stopping, and his stomach was definitely churning – it didn't seem entirely sure of where it was supposed to belong. He grinned at his mother and wobbled across to the ghost train. He had only ridden on it nineteen times, and he wanted to make it up to twenty before the end of the weekend. Besides, he knew exactly what was going to happen, and the fun of the ghost train was watching everyone else scream.

"Hello, young Billy," said Alf, the driver, as Billy tottered up the steps.

"Hello, Alf," said Billy, taking his favourite seat at the back of the train.

From there, he could watch all the other

The Secret Prankster

passengers jumping out of their skins. As the train pulled away from the platform, he reached for the toffee apple in his pocket, picked off the bits of fluff on it and started munching. His stomach still felt a little bit funny, but he hoped that the toffee apple would help. It was fruit, after all.

At first, everything went as normal. The disembodied hand stretched out and touched people.

The skeleton rattled in the corner. The blood-curdling scream made everyone jump. But then something happened that had never happened before. Billy was so surprised that he actually stopped eating his toffee apple.

EEEEEEEK!

The Secret Prankster

When you're on a ghost train, you expect certain things to happen. You expect the train to grind to a halt. You expect cobwebs to tickle your face. You expect to hear the eerie sound of dripping blood.

You don't expect the train driver to scream like a little girl.

But that's exactly what happened. One minute the train was rumbling along as usual. The next minute Alf let out a high-pitched screech and slammed on the brakes, bringing the train to a squealing stop.

"Heeeeeeeeeelp!" he whimpered. "Gh… gh…gh…ghost!"

The other passengers giggled. They all thought that this was part of the ride. Only Billy knew that this had never, ever happened before. He dropped his toffee apple and put his hands on his knees to stop them from knocking together.

Something had appeared out of the gloom beside the driver's seat. It was white and glowing, and it was raising clawed hands above its head.

"WAHHHH!" cried Alf, fainting on the spot.

The Secret Prankster

Billy's mouth had gone completely dry. If you have never been scared enough to experience this, consider yourself very lucky. Billy's tongue felt as if it didn't belong there any more. His heart was making a bid for freedom, and he thought his eyes might pop out of his head. HE WAS SEEING A REAL GHOST!

But then Billy noticed something rather odd. The glowing white ghost was not drifting over the ground in the way that he would expect a spook to behave. Instead, he could see a pair of slippers peeking out from below the white form. Fluffy slippers. Brown fluffy slippers.

Suddenly, Billy's legs didn't feel quite so much like rubber bands. *That's not a ghost!* he thought.

He clambered out of the train and crept along to the front. When he got closer, he could see that the ghostly white glow was actually a large sheet covered in glow-in-the-dark paint. He reached out his hand, grasped the sheet and gave it a hard tug.

"ARGH!" yelled the ghost as the sheet came away in Billy's hand.

Billy stared in utter amazement. The figure under the sheet was dressed in a strange costume patterned with diamond shapes of red and yellow.

The Secret Prankster

It was impossible to tell if it was a man or a woman. Its face was covered with a white mask, and there was a three-cornered hat perched on its head that was made out of the same material as the costume.

"Ha ha!" giggled the figure in a high-pitched, sing-song voice. "Pranked you!"

Then he (or she) threw something on the ground. There was a bright flash and a loud bang.

"SMOKE BOMB!" Billy yelled, coughing.

He reached through the darkness and the smoke to grab the figure, but his hands closed on thin air.

"What's going on?" spluttered Alf, raising his head and looking around, his eyes wide with fear. "Where's the ghost gone?"

"That wasn't a ghost," said Billy grimly. "That was the Secret Prankster!"

***

The next morning, Billy woke up feeling very depressed indeed. Normally, he bounced out of bed and ran downstairs. After all, breakfast was his favourite meal of the day. But right now he wasn't thinking about food.

The Secret Prankster

Billy heard his father get up and lock himself in the bathroom. Mr Bonkers had a very particular morning routine. It ended with him gargling and trying to sing 'Ten Green Bottles' at the same time. Usually it made Billy laugh, but not today.

Mrs Bonkers bustled into Billy's room holding his school uniform on a hanger.

"Up you get," she said. "It's a lovely day."

"No, it isn't," said Billy.

"Nonsense," said Mrs Bonkers. "If you're feeling down you should just count your blessings. That always cheers me up."

Billy glared after her as she left his room.

If anyone has ever told you to count your blessings when you were feeling miserable, you'll know how irritating it is. It's the second most annoying thing that someone can say to you.

Billy didn't want to cheer up. He decided to do the exact opposite of what his mother had said. He stared at the ceiling and counted up all the reasons he had to feel rotten.

- He had failed to catch the Secret Prankster, even when he (or she) was standing right in front of him.
- The ticket to the fairground had run out.
- It was the first day back at school after half-term.
- He hadn't written one word of his holiday homework.

Billy let out a long groan and his sister poked her head around the door.

"Smile!" She grinned. "It *could* be worse."

(In case you were wondering, that is the top most annoying thing that someone can say to you.)

"Go away," said Billy, which was actually quite polite under the circumstances.

Betty disappeared and Billy sighed again. How was he going to explain his lack of homework to Mr Little? He made another list in his mind.

- The dog ate it.
  But Mr Little knows that we don't have a dog.
- My dad ate it.

Hmm. Mr Little might actually believe this. He was there for the Great Sports Day Fiasco last term, when Dad lost control of his bionic legs and helped to catch a pair of escaped cheetahs.

• I've been in a coma for a week.
But what if Mr Little checks with Mum?

• I was too busy having fun.
True, but Mr Little thinks writing about fun is more important than having fun.

Billy swung his legs out of bed. *I'm going to have detention for a month,* he thought. He put on his uniform and went slowly downstairs to the kitchen.

His dad was sitting at the kitchen table, listening to the radio and flicking through a car magazine.

"Morning, Billy!" said Mr Bonkers. "The Secret Prankster struck again overnight.

The Secret Prankster

There's a custard pie balanced on top of every streetlamp in town. You, er, don't know anything about it, I suppose?"

"It wasn't me!"

Billy exclaimed. "I wish it had been! I think the Secret Prankster's brilliant!"

He filled up his bowl with an enormous helping of porridge oats, which made him feel a bit better.

"The boy's gone mad," Mr Bonkers said to his wife as she came in from the hanging the laundry on the washing line. "Seems to think the Secret Prankster's a hero."

Mrs Bonkers looked at the car magazine and frowned. It was open at a picture of a sleek red sports car with a lady in a bikini lying on the bonnet. Mr Bonkers quickly turned the page.

"Right," said Mrs Bonkers. "Breakfast! Billy, how hungry are you, dear? Is it a two pork pie morning or just the one?"

Billy dropped his spoon in his empty dish with a clatter.

"Thanks, Mum," he said. "But I think I've had enough."

Mrs Bonkers's mouth fell open.

Mr Bonkers's eyebrows shot up.

Betty just gawped.

"Are you feeling all right?" Mrs Bonkers asked.

"Yes," said Billy, picking up his school bag. "I just thought I'd get to school early."

His family kept staring.

Mrs Bonkers put her hand on Billy's forehead. "Are you sure you're feeling all right?" she asked.

Billy nodded. His stomach was still rumbling slightly, but he was hoping that if he arrived for school early, it might make Mr Little feel more kindly and forgiving towards him.

"Lordy lorks," said Mrs Bonkers. "Betty, dear, could you walk your brother to school this morning? I think he might be having a funny turn."

Billy and Betty set off together. As they reached the end of their road, a gust of wind blew fiercely down the street. It whipped Betty's hair around her head. It whooshed up Billy's trouser legs and made his kneecaps shiver. And it shook the streetlamp on the corner. Something large, yellow and round tumbled off the top. It landed on a cat underneath with a loud, custardy splash.

"YEEOWWWWL!"

squawked the cat, darting into the nearest hedge.

Billy remembered what his dad had told him about the Secret Prankster, and grinned.

The Secret Prankster

"So, what's really going on, Billy?" asked his older sister. "You haven't eaten such a small breakfast since you were born."

"I have to think up a reason why I didn't do my homework," said Billy. "And it's got to be good."

"Hmm, tough one," said Betty. "How about saying Dad blew it up when he was inventing something?"

"But what if Mr Little checks with Dad?" asked Billy.

"Yep, that could be awkward," Betty agreed.

"I could say you tore it up on purpose, just to spite me," said Billy.

"Mr Little would never believe you," said Betty calmly.

Billy had to admit that this was true. Betty was very well behaved at school.

By the time they reached the school gates, Billy still hadn't thought of one single excuse that Mr Little would have the slightest chance of believing.

"There's only one thing for it," he said. "I'll just have to tell him the truth and hope he's in a good mood."

"Good luck," said Betty with a pitying grin.

Billy couldn't raise a smile in response. He trudged in the direction of his classroom. There were only a few other children in the playground, and he knew that they would all stay outside until the last possible minute.

If you have ever been inside your school when you were supposed to be playing outside, you'll know how different it feels from normal. Your footsteps echo along the corridors. The classrooms are eerily

The Secret Prankster

quiet. And you get that feeling that the headmaster might shout your name at any minute and demand to know what you think you're doing.

Billy found himself tiptoeing and holding his breath. His classroom door was open, so he slipped inside. No one was there, but the door of the storeroom in the corner was slightly ajar.

...e must be getting out some books for ...st lesson, Billy thought.

Billy walked over to the cupboard, running over his apology in his mind. He expected to see Mr Little counting pencils. He expected to see Mr Little flicking through books. But never in his wildest, most candyfloss-fuelled dreams did he expect to see what he saw next.

Mr Little was standing in the middle of the storeroom, taking off the red and yellow outfit that belonged to the Secret Prankster!

"Mr LITTLE!" Billy exclaimed.

The Secret Prankster

His teacher whirled around, lost his balance and fell onto the floor with the outfit around his ankles.

Billy stared at Mr Little.

Mr Little stared at Billy.

There was a long, long, *loooooonnnnnng* pause.

I don't suppose that you would have any idea what to do or say in a situation like that. Billy certainly didn't. He just stood there with his mouth hanging open. In fact, if he had been able to look into a mirror at that moment, he would have seen a striking resemblance to his goldfish, Snapper.

"Ahem," said Mr Little, clearing his throat. "Rumbled! Well, this is unfortunate."

He pulled the costume off from over his usual grey suit and stood up. He smoothed down his hair, put on his glasses and looked at Billy again.

"Close your mouth, Billy," he said. "The flies'll get in."

Billy closed his mouth with a snap, and then opened it again to speak.

"Wh–what . . . Wh–why . . . How—"

Mr Little sighed. "I suppose there's no chance of your forgetting about what you've just seen, is there?" he asked.

Billy shook his head and tried to remember how to string a sentence together. He felt as if he'd just found out that the Earth was made of butterscotch ice cream.

"I might have been able to talk my way out of this if you hadn't seen me last night," Mr Little went on. "It was you in the ghost train, wasn't it?"

Billy nodded and finally found his voice.

"YOU'RE the Secret Prankster?" he asked. "But . . . you're so boring!"

Mr Little narrowed his eyes and Billy gulped.

"Um, what I meant to say was..." he stammered, " . . . er . . . "

"ME, boring?" exclaimed Mr Little. "My goodness, Billy, it's YOU KIDS that are boring!"

"What?" Billy squeaked, hardly able to believe his ears.

"Look, Billy, I'm your teacher," said Mr Little. "I can't encourage naughtiness in the classroom. But you lot are all TOO WELL BEHAVED. It's as if you don't know how to have fun! I never have to confiscate catapults. I never find stink bombs under my desk. And I've never sat on a single whoopee cushion. I had to show you all how to have a bit of fun!"

Slowly, Billy started to smile. His smile grew wider . . . and wider . . . and wider.

"Mr Little, you're a GENIUS!" he said.

"I suppose my fun's over now," said Mr Little sadly. "You won't be able to keep this to yourself, will you?"

I expect you know how tempting it can be to reveal a secret. And I'm sure you know how bad Billy is at resisting temptation.

Billy thought about it for a moment. He imagined telling everyone that Mr Little was the Secret Prankster. He imagined how

The Secret Prankster

funny their surprised faces would look. He imagined how impressed they would be that he had found out the truth.

But then he thought about bananas in car exhausts and jam in Mrs Furball's wig. He thought about porridge bombs and custard pies on the streetlamps. Did he really want to put a stop to all those fantastic tricks?

Billy came to a decision.

"I'm not going to tell anyone!" he declared. "I think it's absolutely brilliant!"

Mr Little looked very relieved. He liked being the Secret Prankster. He also suspected that the headmaster wouldn't see the funny side of it.

"That's great, Billy," he said. "How can I ever thank you?"

Billy's smile grew even wider.

"It's funny that you should ask me that, Mr Little," he said. "You see, there's this little matter of my holiday homework…"

***

Half an hour later, the classroom was packed with children. Mr Little stood at the front of the room, his arms folded. His hair was grey. His suit was grey. Even his tie was grey. He looked very, very, VERY boring.

"Welcome back to another school term," he said in a dull voice. "I hope that you all had a nice half-term holiday?"

"Sir, Sir, Billy Bonkers did, Sir," said William Whipton-Wassett, who was a bit of a know-it-all. "He went to Venice and caught some robbers. EVERYONE'S talking about it."

The Secret Prankster

Billy felt his cheeks go red, and he started to wish that he had eaten a bit more breakfast.

"Really, Billy?" said Mr Little, looking at him. "Well, I'm sure we'd all like to hear about your adventures in Italy. Why don't you come up to the front of the class and tell everyone about it?"

Feeling a little bit shy but also rather proud, Billy stood up and walked to the front of the classroom. Mr Little pulled out his own comfortable padded teacher's chair and put it down behind Billy.

"Sit down and tell us all about it," he said.

Now, if Billy had been paying a little bit more attention, he might have noticed a sparkle in Mr Little's eyes. He might have noticed the faintest, flimsiest shadow of a smile hovering around his teacher's mouth. But he was thinking about his adventures in Venice, and he wasn't paying attention.

THAT was a big mistake.

Before I go on, I think I should warn you that something extremely embarrassing is about to happen. If you blush easily, this is the moment to shuffle into a corner and face the wall. What happened next would be talked about in school for years to come. The story would be told across thirty dinner tables that evening. It would be the first thing that everyone always remembered about Billy Bonkers.

As Billy sat down on the chair, there was a wet, splurting explosion from the general

BLLRRTHP!

direction of his bottom.

There was a breathless moment of silence, and then the entire class fell off their chairs. They clutched their bellies. They wept with laughter. They pointed and shrieked. William Whipton-Wassett came within a whisker of wetting himself.

Billy looked down. The salmon-coloured neck of a whoopee cushion was poking out from under the seat pad.

Whoopee cushion

123

Billy Bonkers

He jumped to his feet and whirled around to face Mr Little, who, in a flash, pulled the whoopee cushion out of sight. And of course no one noticed, because they were all rolling around on the classroom floor, clutching their sides, gasping for breath and laughing hysterically. Billy was helpless. He had been well and truly pranked.

"Everyone stop laughing!" he shouted.

Billy Bonkers

'**Utterly bonkers!
A riot of fun! I loved it!**'
– Harry Enfield

**Mad stuff happens with Billy Bonkers!
Whether he's flying through the air propelled
by porridge power, or blasting headfirst into a
chocolate-covered planet – life is never boring
with Billy, it's BONKERS!**

**Three hilarious stories in one from an award-
winning author and illustrator team.**

978 1 84616 151 3 £4.99 pbk

978 1 40830 357 3 £5.99 pbk

978 1 40831 465 4 £4.99 pbk

ORCHARD BOOKS

www.orchardbooks.co.uk

Max and Molly's Guide To Trouble!

Meet Max and Molly: terrorising the neighbourhood really extremely politely...

Max and Molly's guides guarantee brilliantly funny mayhem and mischief as we learn how to be a genius, catch a criminal, build an abominable snowman and stop a Viking invasion!

978 1 40830 519 5 £4.99 Pbk
978 1 40831 572 9 eBook

978 1 40830 520 1 £4.99 Pbk
978 1 40831 573 6 eBook

978 1 40830 521 8 £4.99 Pbk
978 1 408 31574 3 eBook

978 1 40830 522 5 £4.99 Pbk
978 1 408 31575 0 eBook

Out Augus. 2012